TODAY WE TOOK CHRIS T
SHOPPING.
YVONNE & ME

FEB 1990.
15

THE ADVENTURES
OF
TOM THUMB

First published in Great Britain in 1985 by
Octopus Books Limited

This edition published in 1988 by
Treasure Press
Michelin House
81 Fulham Road
London SW3 6RB

Reprinted 1989

ISBN 1 85051 260 4

Printed by Mandarin Offset in Hong Kong

THE ADVENTURES
— OF —
TOM THUMB

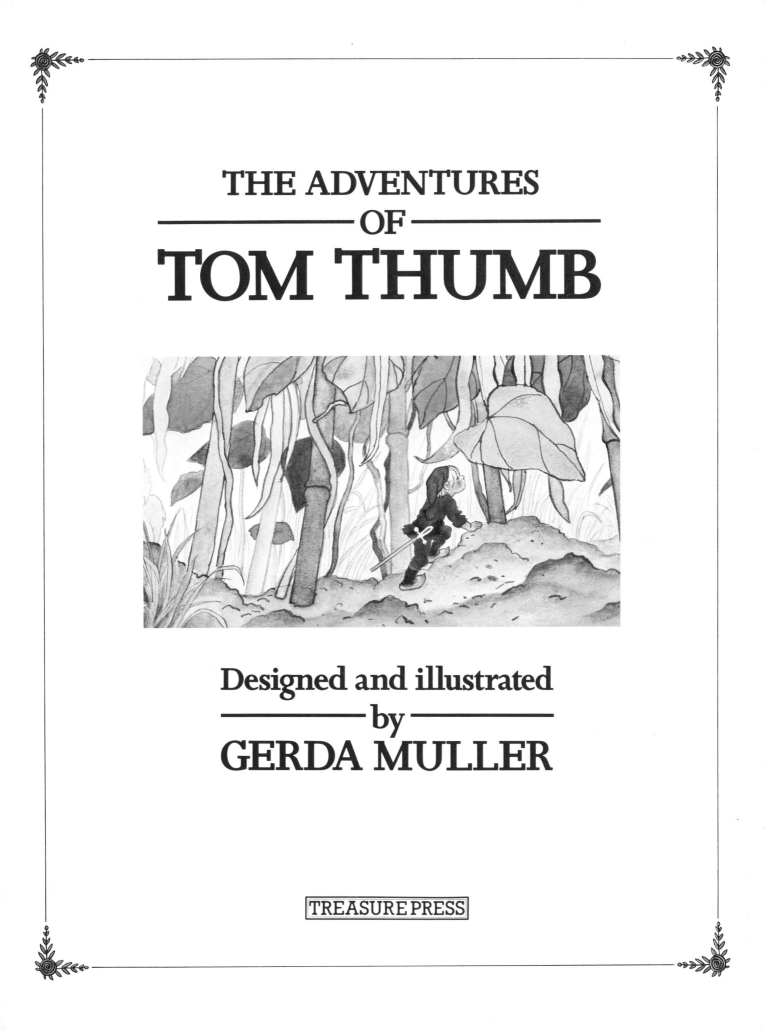

Designed and illustrated
— by —
GERDA MULLER

TREASURE PRESS

Once upon a time a countryman and his wife lived in a small cottage at the edge of a village. All they possessed was a field which the farmer cultivated, a horse, a cow, several chickens and some rabbits.

They were not rich, but they were contented with their lot, and if only they had had a child they would have been perfectly happy.

'Ah,' sighed the farmer's wife, as she was peeling the potatoes one day for their supper, 'how I would love to have a little boy, even if he was no bigger than my finger.'

The magician Merlin, who happened to be passing by, heard her. And, as he was a kind man, he decided to make the good woman's wish come true. Unless you happen to be a magician it is not easy, is it, to fulfil a wish like that?

Merlin went to look for a fairy called Mopsa, who agreed to help him. Days passed, then weeks. Summer came. The harvest was gathered in. In September the yellow gorse flowered for the second time in the year. The birds gorged themselves on the red berries of the hawthorn and on the black fruit of the elderberry.

Each day the farmer went to work in his field.

On this particular morning some violet-blue flowers had burst open at the tops of the stalks of artichokes which had not been harvested.

A light wind was blowing and the artichokes bent their heads in response to it. But one of the stalks bent more heavily than the rest. Curious, the peasant went up to it. And in the centre of the flower he discovered a tiny child, curled up and fast asleep.

Taking care not to awaken the child, the man plucked the flower and returned home with it as fast as he could.

When his wife saw the tiny boy which fate had brought them, she was overjoyed. The happy pair marvelled at their good fortune.

But still, the child was scarcely as big as your thumb. So that was how they came to call him Tom Thumb.

Tom Thumb's mother made him a cradle out of an old clog, which she padded with cotton wool so as to keep him warm.

Small as he was, Tom Thumb was perfectly proportioned, and while he hardly grew any bigger, his intelligence developed fast. He soon showed himself to be a lively boy.

When he was still only one he could already talk fluently, and he ran about wherever his little legs would carry him.

His mother made him a red suit from one of her old handkerchiefs, and he had a blue cap which suited him to perfection.

His father fashioned a pair of clogs for him from a willow wand and, as you may well imagine, his parents were really proud of his appearance.

To complete his turn-out, Mopsa, his fairy godmother, gave him a little sword made from a well-sharpened embroidery needle. This sword was to prove very valuable to Tom Thumb when he had to face the many dangers to which his small size made him liable – as we shall see.

Nothing was greater fun than to watch little Tom busying himself each day.

The village carpenter made a set of furniture the right size for him. He sat on a tiny chair of plaited straw in front of a little polished oak table on which his mother served him his meals.

Amongst her old toys, his mother found a tiny dolls' tea set which suited Tom perfectly.

A teaspoon of soup, a mouthful of meat, a dab of potato, the half of the quarter of an apple cut up into thin slices: these made an excellent meal which Tom ate with lively pleasure. What he liked best of all, though, was his Sunday tartlet. His mother always set a juicy raspberry or a blackberry in the middle.

Tom Thumb was a good little fellow and he was far from lazy. After each meal he brushed up the crumbs that had fallen from the table with a brush made from dried blades of grass. When the farmer's wife did her sewing, he threaded her needle for her.

Tom's father made a little garden for him in a flower pot and in it he put a strawberry plant and the seeds of some tiny flowers. Every morning he presented his mother with a strawberry, a daisy or a violet, which he placed beside her bowl at breakfast. Sometimes the farmer took his son with him in his pocket when he went to the fields. They chatted together gaily as he worked.

There came a time when Tom was able to walk by himself in his parents' vegetable garden.

Because he was so small he found it hard to make his way through the tomato plants, the cauliflowers and the rows of haricot beans to the part of the garden he wished to reach. Here his mother cultivated her flowers, and roses grew side-by-side with daisies

and hydrangeas. For Tom Thumb a mound of earth was a hill, an artichoke stem an enormous tree, a tuft a small wood. But that wasn't all he had to contend with.

At every step he took, Tom Thumb met danger.

One day a beetle very nearly caught him in its claws. Another time a slug which he had not spotted almost crushed him.

One afternoon, when he had fallen asleep under a rose bush, Tom Thumb was awakened by a terrible buzzing which filled the air around him.

Zooming towards him was an enormous wasp! He only just escaped from it by rolling on his side.

Tom was very brave. He got up and grasped hold of the little sword which his godmother had given him. The wasp attacked him again. Tom Thumb stood firm and stabbed at it, making it hesitate. But the infuriated insect would not admit defeat.

It started to circle round Tom Thumb, trying to reach him with its sting. Tom made one or two thrusts with his sword, which flashed in the sun. Dazzled, the wasp stopped circling and for a moment hung motionless in the air.

That was its undoing. Tom planted his sword in its body and the insect fell dead to the ground.

Tom Thumb had had such a shock that he was still trembling when he reached home again. His mother gave him a mug of hot chocolate to help him to calm down.

Tom Thumb quickly learned to read and to write with a tiny pen which his father made for him. But the words he wrote in his exercise book were so small that they could not be read without a magnifying glass.

Tom Thumb loved to draw. He often drew.

my a teacher

He drew portraits: his father's, his mother's, one of the teacher who made little books of the right size for him, and one of Mopsa, his godmother.

He drew the horse and the cow, the woodpecker who lived in the wood close by, the oriole who gorged herself each spring on the cherries in the garden, the winter countryside with its bare trees.

Tom also made a fine picture of his fight with the wasp.

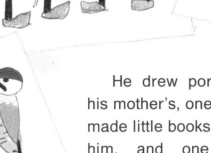

No doubt because he was so small, Tom Thumb had a very keen sense of hearing and he was able to make out sounds which could not be heard by ordinary ears. In addition, he could easily understand the language of the animals and as a result he was able to do his father a great service.

It had rained all one night. But in the middle of the morning the sun appeared and Tom decided to go for a walk. He buckled on his sword, put on his blue cap and went out. He made for the part of the garden where the lettuces grew.

On the way he suddenly heard a strange conversation. It was between two snails, who were chatting together. Tom Thumb listened to what they were saying.

'Do you know, my friend,' said one, 'how delicious the lettuces are this year? I tasted one last night and had a regular feast off it.'

'Could you show me where it is?' the other asked. 'I am new here and I don't know where to find the lettuce bed.'

'Of course,' replied the snail who had spoken first. 'Follow me. We shall be there before nightfall.' And the two friends set off together. They had a long way to go – long at least for snails!

Tom Thumb ran home. But his father was working in the fields and would not be back until late afternoon.

'Father! Father!' Tom Thumb called out from a distance, as soon as he saw him. 'Come quickly! Your lettuces are going to be eaten up tonight.'

'What's that you're saying?' answered his father, smiling. 'Don't talk rubbish and go home at once. I'm hungry and it is nearly supper time.'

'But father!' said Tom Thumb. 'I overheard two snails talking about it this morning. Hurry, or they will eat the lot.'

Tom Thumb's father thought at first that he was joking, but Tom was so insistent that in the end he decided to go to the vegetable garden with him.

The two snails had already eaten up one lettuce and were greedily starting on another one. How they were enjoying themselves with the tender leaves!

As you can imagine, the farmer lost no time in putting an end to their feast. And the chickens were very pleased at having two fresh, fat snails for their dinner!

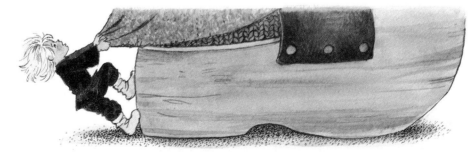

Tom Thumb did not have only good points. He also had one very bad one: he was curious. The poor fellow was well punished for his curiosity, and this is how it came about.

One morning, when his mother had gone to the village to do some shopping, Tom Thumb climbed up on to the table. In a bowl covered by a piece of paper some pancake mixture was standing ready.

Tom wanted to find out what was in the bowl. To help himself reach the rim he climbed up a fork which he found there. But no sooner had he raised the piece of paper than he slipped and plunged headlong into the bowl.

His mother, who returned just at that moment, saw something

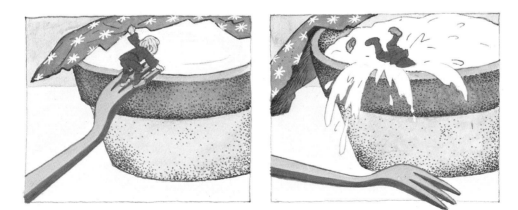

moving violently about in the mixture. She thought it must be a mouse which had fallen in. She seized the bowl and threw its contents, including Tom, out of the window.

A miller was passing by, singing with his mouth wide open. The contents of the bowl flew right into his gaping mouth, and he swallowed the lot in a single gulp.

The surprised miller, rubbing his stomach with pleasure at this unexpected treat, continued on his way. His donkey trotted briskly along and they were soon some distance from the village.

But, when he wanted to start singing again, the miller had a fright. No sound came out of his throat, but instead he felt an unpleasant tickling.

When he reached home the miller lay down, feeling really ill.

The miller's wife asked all the doctors in the neighbourhood to visit him. But they did not understand this strange illness at all.

The miller complained of having a frog in his throat which nothing would clear. The doctors gave him ointments, cough syrups and gargles, but right in the middle of their treatment the miller was overcome by a violent fit of coughing.

Tom Thumb, who as you may imagine was not feeling very happy in the miller's throat, was suddenly thrown out into the air.

He came down on the bed of the miller, who was truly astonished, as you may well believe. The doctors were not too pleased, because they felt they had been made to look silly. They went away, but not before they had been well paid for being so upset.

The miller, furious at what had happened, grasped hold of Tom Thumb and tossed him into the stream that flowed beneath the window of the mill.

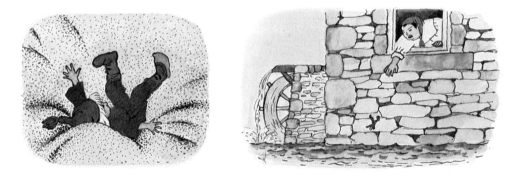

It was apparently Tom's fate always to be swallowed by someone or other. A big fish, who was swimming next to the mill-wheel, spied the little creature violently moving his arms, took him for some kind of water-insect, and gobbled him up.

After that the fish swam to a quiet pool, where he was caught by some fishermen. Seeing what a monster they had captured, they took it to the king's cook.

Just imagine the cook's surprise when, on opening up the fish, he found Tom Thumb! Tom was overjoyed at finding himself in the open air once again. The cook almost thought he had stuck his knife into a whale and that it was Jonah himself who stood before him!

Tom Thumb had been well brought up. Taking off his blue cap he made the cook a bow and said: 'Sir Cook, you have just done me an extremely good turn and I should like to thank you.'

Astonished by such a prodigy, the cook decided to take Tom Thumb to his master. He knocked at the door of the royal apartment. The king was still asleep and the guards wanted the cook to go away. However, he was so insistent that in the end they woke the king up. When the king saw Tom Thumb he was astonished.

'Bless my soul!' exclaimed the king. 'I've never seen anyone so small in my whole life. Do you come from the kingdom of Lilliput?'

Tom told the king his story. He finished by saying, 'I should be very happy if I could return to my parents. They must be worried at my absence.'

The king invited Tom Thumb to stay for some time at the palace and he promised to write to his parents that very day to tell them that their son was well. In the meantime he commanded a servant to carry Tom Thumb to the queen, to entertain her.

Alas, after drinking a cup of hot chocolate and eating a roll, the king became so taken up with affairs of state that he completely forgot his promise. Tom meanwhile was amusing the queen, who loved to watch him.

The queen commanded His Majesty's tailor to make a court costume for Tom Thumb. After all the adventures he had had, his old clothes were wearing out and were even torn in some places, so he badly needed something new to wear.

The tailor made a doublet of Italian velvet and a pair of breeches of sky-blue silk. The costume was completed by a shirt of delicate lace, white stockings and shoes with gilt buckles. A hat with a feather in it and a sword gave Tom Thumb the air of a fine gentleman.

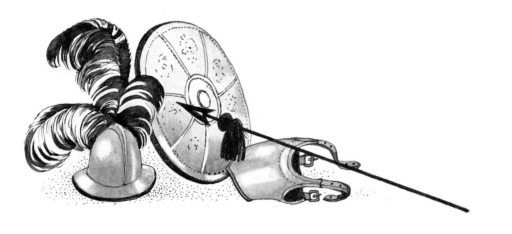

The royal armourer made him a suit of armour and a helmet exactly right for his size, so that Tom Thumb now had a wardrobe as complete as that of any of the gentlemen of the court.

Reassured by the king's promise to write to his parents, Tom Thumb was, at first, happy to amuse himself with these novelties. He was proud to strut up and down in front of the courtiers, many of whom came to admire him.

But, after a while Tom had had enough of pirouetting and bowing for the entertainment of the courtiers.

Then the queen, who had grown really fond of Tom Thumb, had a good idea. She ordered the royal carpenter to make him a miniature house. On the ground floor was a sitting room with comfortable easy chairs in which Tom could sit. Beside it was a library filled with tiny, specially-printed books.

On the first floor was a bedroom with a four-poster bed and a toilet table. There Tom could rest whenever he felt like it. The attic was furnished as a games room and every game Tom could wish for was there. He didn't play with them much, however; everyone soon tires of playing alone.

In this house Tom Thumb was safe from the prying eyes of visitors. He would obey only the King's commands.

The king often came to see Tom Thumb because he found it boring to be always reading documents of state. To distract him, he told Tom to do cartwheels and pirouettes and to dance. While Tom was glad to entertain the king, he did not like acting the buffoon for him all the time. And, so far from his parents, Tom began to find the time hang heavily.

'Since they won't write to me,' he said to himself one day, 'I shall have to write a letter to them.'

Tom went into his library. He sat down at his desk, took a sheet of paper no bigger than a postage stamp and a pen as fine as a needle, and he wrote:

Dear Parents,
You must miss me a lot. When are you coming to fetch me?
I am waiting for you impashently.
Your son
Tom Thumb

When the ink was dry, Tom folded the sheet, put it into a tiny envelope, and ran to the castle battlements to find a servant to take charge of the letter.

No one was there. Tom Thumb put a pebble into the envelope and tossed it from the battlements.

'Someone will find my letter and will see that it reaches my parents,' he thought. Then he returned home, satisfied with what he had done.

Every day Tom watched out for his parents. He was sure they would come to look for him as soon as they received his letter.

The queen saw that he was bored. She gave him a drawing book to amuse him.

Tom Thumb entertained himself by drawing everything round about him: the palace, the furnishings of his little house, the views from the battlements, and also the courtiers, the palace servants, and everyone he met.

The king asked to see these drawings. He examined them closely and was much amused. Tom Thumb's portraits, it must be admitted, were sometimes far from flattering. Some of them have been preserved in the royal archives. Here they are:

The courtiers whose portraits were unflattering thought that Tom Thumb was making fun of them and so they came to hate him. They would not have minded if some disaster had happened to him.

So it was that when, one day, in the course of a royal hunt, a cat pounced on the field mouse which served Tom as a steed, and carried it and its rider up to the branch of a tree, not a single one of the courtiers went to help him.

Tom was in a tight spot.

No one had gone to tell the king of the grave danger that was threatening his little friend. By the time the king realised that he had disappeared, Tom was bravely fighting the cat.

He had drawn his sword and was fighting with all his might. In the end he gave such a fierce thrust that the cat ran off, leaving the mouse behind.

But the poor field mouse was already dead. Tired out, Tom swayed and fell off the branch at the very moment when the king was hastening to his aid. The king had only just time enough to hold out his hat; Tom fell *plop* right into it.

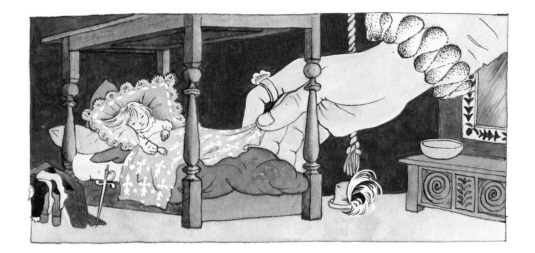

Tom was so worn out by his fight with the cat that he fell ill. The queen looked after him with tender care. She herself prepared hot drinks for him and every day she also gave him a cordial to restore his strength. None of this helped. Feeling that he was dying, Tom Thumb sighed and said:

'Ah! How I should like to see my mother and father for one last time!'

Mopsa, his fairy godmother, had been watching over him since he was born and now she hastened to help him.

She had intended to cure Tom of his curiosity once and for all, but seeing that he was now so ill, she decided to call a halt to his ordeal. After all, it was not really the poor fellow's fault.

She went to look for the queen and told her that Tom should return to his parents as quickly as possible. Unless he did so, he would surely die. The queen agreed to the separation on condition that he should visit her again when he was better. His godmother promised that he would surely do so.

At her command there appeared a carriage drawn by four dragonflies, and in it Tom was carried to where his godmother lived. The fairy wished to care for him until he was well enough to return to his parents.

In the kingdom of the fairies Tom at once began to recover, and soon he had regained his strength. Mopsa took him to the treasure chamber of her palace. Gold coins of every size filled the room.

'You may now return to your parents,' said the fairy. 'But first, choose whatever you like from here.'

She wanted to test Tom's goodness of heart and to see what sacrifice he was willing to make out of love of his parents.

Tom, good son that he was, knew that his parents were not rich and that a gold coin would make them happy. So, in spite of the trouble it would cause him, he chose the biggest coin he could carry, and with a great effort he heaved it onto his back. Then he said farewell to his godmother and went on his way.

The journey to the village was a long one. Tom had to make his way along muddy tracks, and through a thick wood where branches scratched him as he passed. He had to climb a hill and descend a steep slope on the other side.

Because of the weight of the coin, Tom's breath came in great gasps. But never for a moment did he consider putting the coin down. He thought of the joy it would bring his parents and he bravely struggled on.

From time to time he stopped to wipe his forehead, but soon he went on again.

Now Tom stumbled at each step. He could go no further. Placing the coin on its side he trundled it like a hoop, and in this way he made some progress. But the coin was heavy. It overbalanced and nearly crushed Tom as it fell. Once again he heaved it onto his back and continued on his way.

As dusk approached Tom saw a thread of smoke rising behind some pine trees. He knew he was not far from home. Soon he could make out the big oak tree and the roof of the house.

Then he saw his father and mother hastening towards him with their arms outstretched. Merlin the magician, to whom Mopsa had told everything, had decided that Tom had been tested severely enough and had himself gone to warn Tom's parents of their son's return.

Tom Thumb gave his parents a hundred kisses. His father put the gold coin in one pocket and his son in the other, and, chattering joyfully, they went indoors.

From time to time Tom Thumb paid a visit to the king and queen, but he never stayed with them for more than a day or two before returning home where his parents were waiting for him. The three of them lived together happily for many, many years.

If you should one day pass close to their village you may see, at the edge of a field, three pine trees pointing towards the sky. Next to them the little house with closed shutters belongs to Tom Thumb. You will recognise its grey walls, shaded by a big oak tree. You will hear the tapping of a woodpecker on the knotty trunk. Perhaps you will see the yellow flash of an oriole as it passes, gorged with cherries. But walk carefully.

Tom Thumb might be lying hidden under a leaf or behind a blade of grass, or sleeping beneath a cluster of bluebells.